T7P

MW01278184

TIPS FOR SUCCESS™

TOP 10 TIPS FOR ETHICAL LIVING AND GOOD CITIZENSHIP

JOE CRAIG

ROSEN
PUBLISHING®

NEW YORK

Published in 2013 by The Rosen Publishing Group, Inc.
29 East 21st Street, New York, NY 10010

Copyright © 2013 by The Rosen Publishing Group, Inc.

First Edition

Library of Congress Cataloging-in-Publication Data

Craig, Joe.
Top 10 tips for ethical living and good citizenship/Joe Craig.—1st ed.
    p. cm.—(Tips for success)
Includes bibliographical references (p.   ) and index.
ISBN 978-1-4488-6864-3 (library binding)
1. Conduct of life. 2. Citizenship. I. Title.
BJ1595.C75 2013
170'.44—dc23

                                                            2011052589

Manufactured in the United States of America

CPSIA Compliance Information: Batch #S12YA: For further information, contact Rosen Publishing, New York, New York, at 1-800-237-9932.

CONTENTS

INTRODUCTION

We are social animals. When we are born, there is very little that we know. Unlike other animals, which are born with strong instincts, we humans must learn how to live socially. We learn this from the people around us. As a result, we're closely linked to the community in which we're raised. Our daily lives and identities are affected by the experiences that we share with the people in our community. We learn the community's values, history, and rules. When we become part of a community, it also becomes a part of us.

Citizenship is the state of being a citizen—a member, a resident—within a community. A citizen is someone who lives in and belongs to a community and participates in and contributes to its civic life. As citizens, we enjoy certain rights, but we also shoulder certain responsibilities. To be good citizens, we must live up to these responsibilities. That's because we share the community with its other members. Our actions affect other members of the community, and theirs affect us. We always have to consider the well-being of the entire community. We must work for its continued health, safety, and prosperity, now and into the future. A community can only grow and flourish through time if good citizens do their best to improve it. Being a good citizen means being proactive.

Good citizens must also live ethically, or morally. We all have a sense of right and wrong, but we don't always follow our best judgment. Whenever we decide

Students plant a public garden. Their hard work will benefit the entire community.

not to live ethically, we risk hurting the people around us and ourselves, and the community as a whole suffers. That's not to say we can't personally benefit from living ethically and being good citizens. Being a good citizen has immediate rewards. Ethical living and good citizenship improve academic, professional, and social success and boost happiness and quality of life. By being good citizens and living ethically, we encourage others to do the same.

They'll return the favor to us, and we'll receive long-term benefits within a well-ordered, civil, and prosperous society.

This book provides ten tips on how to be a good citizen and live ethically. Taken together, they are the basic toolkit you will need to thrive and prosper in the wider world and help create a smoothly functioning, fair, and welcoming society in which each of its members can thrive and prosper.

We're all part of an enormous web of relationships that covers the entire world. It's virtually impossible for any human being to be completely alone or truly live apart from a community. We're all part of religious, ethnic, and ideological communities. We're part of the communities in which we we live—town, state, and country—and we're even part of a global community. Different communities have different levels of intimacy, but when we're a part of a community, we're connected to all of its other members.

Being a good and ethical citizen of these various communities means understanding how we're connected to others and doing our best to consider the good of all before we act or speak. It might be difficult to see, but you share commonalities with people all around the neighborhood, the town, the state, the country, and the world. Their well-being is, in many respects, your well-being.

STUDY
ETHICS 101

Ethics, or morals, are principles that guide our actions. For example, we know that it's wrong to lie, so we don't (or try hard not to, in most cases). It's not always easy to do what's right, however. In fact, it's often difficult. That doesn't mean there aren't rewards—we all benefit from living ethically. Let's look at some simple ethical principles and examine how they better our lives.

DO NO HARM

Do no harm. Don't hurt others. This rule means more than not physically harming another person. It means doing absolutely no harm—none—whether intentionally or unintentionally, physically, emotionally, verbally, or otherwise. It doesn't just extend to other people, but also to all living things, the environment, property,

Whether physical or verbal in nature, bullying does serious harm. That's why these students proudly signed a no-bullying pledge.

and yourself. Fighting, stealing, littering, vandalism, bullying, cyberbullying, and name-calling are all ways of doing harm, so you should never engage in such activity. The way you treat others determines the way they'll treat you, for better or worse—if you hurt them, they'll likely hurt you back.

We rely on the people and things around us for our well-being, sometimes in ways that aren't easy to see. The environment, for example, provides us with food, water, air, and everything we need to live a healthy life. By harming it, we harm ourselves. The same goes for people. By harming another person, you reduce the

GOOD INTENTIONS

Ethics guide us in our daily life. However, certain situations can be morally complicated, and it isn't always easy to decide what's right and what's wrong. For example, is lying wrong if you're telling an untruth to protect someone else's feelings? We all occasionally get into situations in which our ethical principles don't provide any easy answers. What do we do in such cases?

Some people believe that we should judge right and wrong based not only on the specific action, but also on the intention. Intentions are the reasons a person does something. There are many different reasons why a person might lie—to avoid guilt, to hurt another person, to get someone into or keep someone out of trouble, or to protect another person's feelings. Although lying is ethically wrong, perhaps we could allow a lie depending on the person's reason for lying, or the intention behind his or her lie.

Throughout life, we will encounter situations that test our ethical code. Sometimes it might be difficult to decide what's right and what's wrong. Keep pure intentions, and do your best to follow your moral code.

likelihood that the person will ever offer you help when you need it. Plus, if you're caught fighting, stealing, bullying, or doing harm in any way, you'll be punished. It may seem like it's easy to get away with doing harm without punishment, but people usually get caught sooner or later.

BE HONEST

Be honest—don't lie or cheat. You might think lying doesn't hurt anyone, but it does. The people in your life expect you to be honest. They trust you, and if you violate that trust, you'll lose it, possibly forever. Trust is an important part of any relationship, and it's very difficult to regain someone's trust once it's lost. By being dishonest, you can permanently damage your family relationships, friendships, and personal connections.

BE FAIR

Be fair. Fairness means treating everyone justly and equally, free from any prejudice. Being treated unfairly is one of the worst experiences one can have. And unfair treatment hurts even those who benefit from it. Anyone who benefits from someone else being treated unfairly can't feel good about what they've been given or what they've won because it wasn't truly earned by their own merit or actions. If you want others to be fair to you, it's important that you be fair to them. Even if it makes things a little harder for you, you will benefit in the long run.

THE GOLDEN RULE

Each of these ethical principles are aspects of the Golden Rule—treat others the same way that you want to be treated. The Golden Rule is also called the ethic of reciprocity, or mutual exchange. It means that you exchange equal treatment with the people you interact with. You wouldn't want to be called names or lied to, so don't do those things to other people. If you aren't sure how to act, refer back to and follow the Golden Rule. Think about whether or not you'd want someone to treat you the way you're treating others. If we all follow the Golden Rule, we'll all be treated fairly.

CONSIDER THE CONSEQUENCES OF YOUR ACTIONS

Every action has consequences. An action is like a stone tossed into a still pond. It creates ripples that spread far beyond the place where the stone hit the water. Actions, too, have a ripple effect, and the consequences can be both far-reaching and unexpected. You're responsible for the consequences of your actions, even if they're unintentional. That's why it's very important to think hard about all possible consequences before acting and possibly making a bad choice.

Have you ever been surprised by the consequences of your actions? We all have. After all, it's impossible to know the future or anticipate the complex chain reaction of cause-and-effect. Learn from your past mistakes and successes when considering future actions. If you know how easy it is to cause an unwanted,

ENVIRONMENTAL CONSEQUENCES

Our actions affect plants, animals, and all of nature, too. Negative consequences of human activity can be obvious, like when someone litters or an oil tanker ruptures and pollutes a large swath of ocean and coastline. But there are also many less dramatic, more subtle, everyday negative environmental impacts. For example, you might not think it's a big deal to leave the faucet running when you brush your teeth, but a running tap wastes almost 2.5 gallons (9.5 liters) of water a minute. Water is scarce in many parts of the United States and the world, so a running tap wastes a valuable resource. It also costs your parents money. If it's hot water that is coming out of the faucet, electricity is being wasted, too.

Most of us don't know where our home's electricity comes from. Many regions rely on coal- or oil-powered plants to generate their energy. Both coal and oil are fossil fuels that, when burned, pollute the environment and emit heat-trapping gases into the atmosphere, resulting in global warming and climate change. The more electricity you use, the more pollution and carbon emissions are created and the more the environment is negatively affected. As harmless as it seems, wasting electricity has consequences.

Our future is tied to the health of our environment. It's best to conserve energy and water whenever possible. If you'd like to know more about the environmental consequences of our actions, visit the U.S. Environmental Protection Agency's Web site (http://www.epa.gov/students). Not only will you help protect the environment, but you'll also help protect our future.

unexpected consequence that is both harmful and impossible to undo, do your best to live ethically. Unethical actions are considered unethical partly because they bring negative consequences to the people around you and to yourself. By steering clear of negative actions, you can help avoid most negative consequences.

CHEATING

Even if we expect certain negative consequences from our actions, we aren't always able to determine how those negative consequences can affect others. Let's say, for example, that you decide to cheat on a test. Worst-case scenario, you get caught and get in trouble, but you didn't study and cheating doesn't hurt anyone anyway, right? It's a victimless crime, isn't it?

Wrong. Your teacher might catch you by noticing the similarities between your test and the test of a person you copied. If he or she does, your teacher will punish both you and the person you copied from, even if that person had nothing to do with it. How can your teacher be sure who cheated off of whom? That student would, and should, blame you and choose not to associate with you anymore. Besides being punished, you'd lose your teacher's and your parents' trust, which is much more important than one test grade.

Even if you aren't caught, by not studying you'll cheat yourself out of truly learning a subject. This lack of knowledge may come back to haunt you later when trying to pass the class, score well on SATs, or get into college. And cheating once can encourage more cheating. If you cheat on one test, you might have to cheat again

If you feel you're not prepared for a test, ask for help from a teacher, tutor, classmate, older sibling, or parent.

when that test's material reappears, such as on a final exam. The more frequently you cheat, the more likely you'll get caught.

If you don't think you're prepared for a test, tell someone, like your parents or a teacher. Maybe a family member, teacher, or fellow student can tutor you. Ask a classmate who is getting good grades to form a study group with you. By studying together, you might even make a new friend.

STEALING

All unethical, negative actions, no matter how harmless they seem, have negative consequences—not just for you, but for others also. Have you ever thought about stealing a candy bar from a store? It doesn't seem like a big deal. After all, candy bars don't cost very much. The store owner won't miss it and can afford the loss of a couple of dollars. But if you're caught stealing, you could get into serious trouble, not just with your parents and the store, but also with the police. Even if you aren't caught, there are consequences. The store owner could punish the clerk for not catching you or blame someone else for the theft. If you don't steal in the first place, you won't hurt anyone—yourself most especially.

It's very difficult to consider all the consequences of your actions, but that's no excuse—negligence is just another form of selfishness and laziness. Think hard, and do your best to create positive consequences.

TIP #3

BE A GOOD NEIGHBOR

To be a good citizen, you must be a good neighbor. A neighbor isn't just someone who lives near someone else. A neighbor is also a person who is kind and helpful toward all human beings, whether they live near or far away. If someone calls you "neighborly," they're complimenting your generosity, kindness, helpfulness, and thoughtfulness.

GIVE AND TAKE

Why should we be good neighbors? Can't we just go home and shut the door behind us? We can, but it wouldn't be in our best interest. Friendly neighbors might resent your unwillingness to socialize. Being on bad terms with your neighbors can actually make your life more difficult, not less. Being on good terms has many, many benefits.

Being a good neighbor isn't completely selfless. For one thing, being a good neighbor is an excellent way to make friends. When you're young, you don't always have the freedom or mobility to travel to your friends' houses when you want to. But if you have friends in your neighborhood, you won't need to travel anywhere. When you want to socialize, play a game, or have fun, all you'll have to do is walk outside.

When you're friendly toward your neighbors, they'll return the favor. Friendly neighbors can help you and your family

A neighborhood watch sign warns potential criminals. Good neighbors watch out for each other, and that makes for a safer community.

in numerous ways. They can pick you up from school when your parents are too busy, or watch your pets when you're out of town. And when you share with them, they'll share with you. Maybe your neighbors will let you use their pool or basketball hoop in exchange for helping them with yard work.

Being a good neighbor will also make you feel more secure. Good neighbors watch out for each other. Yours will be there to protect your property and help you out if something goes wrong. Coming home after school to a friendly, secure environment will also make you feel safer, happier, and more comfortable.

OUR OTHER NEIGHBORS

People aren't our only neighbors. Schools, stores, religious institutions, police and fire departments, and other community organizations and institutions are all neighbors in a sense. We would like them to be good neighbors to us, so we should be good neighbors to them by respecting their role in our community and their right to be a part of it. Patronize local businesses whenever possible. They provide more than just goods and services, but also a local identity that's invaluable to a community. A community with thriving stores tends to be more vibrant, more prosperous, and safer. Police officers and firefighters risk their lives to protect our communities and thus deserve our utmost respect and gratitude.

Local plants and animals are your neighbors, too. Consider the fact that before your city or town was built, it was a natural area without the presence of any human beings. Though certain animals like raccoons, opossums, snakes, deer, and bears may seem like a nuisance, they were the area's original inhabitants, and their habitats have been squeezed and endangered by our presence. They have every right to be there and should not be treated with disrespect or disregard.

It's almost as if being a good neighbor makes your home bigger. You'll be as comfortable and secure in your neighborhood as you are at home.

THE GOOD NEIGHBOR POLICY

You need to be a good neighbor in order to have good neighbors. Start by talking to your neighbors. Introduce yourself. At the very least, smile, say hello, and wave to neighbors when you see them.

It's important to respect your neighbors' needs even when you are on your own property or within your own house. If you know that a neighbor works at night, try to be quiet during the day while he or she is sleeping. Don't play music too loudly with the windows open. If your family is having a party, hold it on a weekend night or make sure it ends early, and be sure to invite your neighbors or at least notify them about it ahead of time.

Keep your yard neat and well cared for as a sign of respect to your neighbors and neighborhood.

Help your parents keep your front yard clean and neat. Your neighbors will appreciate it. Unkempt gardens are unsightly, and weeds can spread into your neighbors' yards. If you live in an apartment, be aware of shared walls, floors, or ceilings. Your neighbors might be able to hear you, so consider their schedule when playing music, watching television, exercising, or having friends over. Ask your parents to invite the neighbors over for coffee or a dinner party.

Being a good neighbor doesn't just involve the people who live around you, but everyone you come into contact with. Be a good neighbor to everyone you interact with. That means always being kind, friendly, thoughtful, and helpful.

TAKE ADVANTAGE OF EVERY OPPORTUNITY TO MAKE FRIENDS

We interact with many different people every day. Often these people will be strangers or acquaintances, maybe your school principal, a clerk at a store, your barber, a neighbor, or your mail carrier. It's in your best interest to be kind to these people and treat them well because every relationship holds the potential for friendship.

FRIENDSHIP NETWORKS

To be friends with people means caring about them for their sake. We're closer with our friends than with anyone else. We share

HEALTH BENEFITS OF FRIENDSHIP

Scientists are only now starting to realize the physical and mental health benefits of friendship. Recently, researchers conducted a study of thirty-four students at the University of Virginia. They took the students to the base of a hill and gave them heavy backpacks. Then the researchers asked the students to guess how steep the hill was. Some students stood in groups, while others stood alone. The students who stood grouped with their friends guessed that the hill was much less steep than did the solitary students. The groups of students who'd been friends the longest offered the lowest estimate of the hill's steepness.

What do these results mean? Perhaps people feel stronger, more confident, and less daunted with their friends because they know they have someone to turn to and upon whom they can rely in a pinch. They feel they can share any burden or challenge, rather than being forced to go it alone. To these people, any challenge—in this case, the steepness of the hill—doesn't seem as looming as it does to people who are alone. Conversely, solitary or lonely people have a harder time dealing with stress than do those individuals who are plugged into a friendship network. This stress can actually damage their health. Loneliness has been linked to heart problems, viral infections, and a shorter lifespan. The beneficial effects of friendship are still being studied, but it is clear that friends are actually good for our health.

secrets with them, have fun with them, and support them, simply because we like and care about them. And we benefit from our friends because they return the favor. They provide support when we need it and countless hours of joy. Everyone needs friends. We should take every opportunity to make more.

Of course, friendship isn't about quantity—one good friend is worth more than a hundred passing acquaintances. But one friendship can lead to more. Our friends have friends, and their friends have friends, and so on and so on. By making friends with just one person, we become part of a much larger web of friendship. Just one friend connects us to countless others.

Technology is changing the way we meet and interact with friends. Social networks and technology make it even more convenient to create new friendships based on common friends and interests. Today, it's easier than ever to make and keep in touch

Social networking sites make it easy to maintain older friendships—especially those that are long distance—and forge new ones with people who share your interests and enthusiasms.

with friends. We can use instant messages, text messages, e-mails, and social networks to plan and organize events with our friends. New technologies make it easy to stay in touch with friends who live all around the country and even the world.

CREATING A COMMUNITY OF FRIENDS

We love our friends, but how is making friends part of good citizenship? Friendship benefits the entire community because having

A friendship with one person can quickly involve you in a larger web of nurturing and supportive friends and acquaintances.

23

friends, even just one friend, makes it easier for us to care about all other people. That's because a friend can show us the great potential for our relationships. If we love our friends, who once were strangers, it will be easier for us to be open toward current strangers who could be future friends. It's impossible to be friends with everyone around us, but if we approach people in a spirit of friendship, we will always get better results from our interactions.

It's not always easy to make friends. In fact, it can be scary to even try because in order to make a new friend, we have to open ourselves up to a certain degree. This makes us vulnerable. We're afraid the other person might resist our friendship, reject us, and hurt our feelings. It takes a lot of strength to open yourself up to a new friend, but the rewards far outweigh the costs. Isn't a new friend worth the risk? All you can do is your best, and it's likely that other good, friendly people will be attracted to you. No matter how it seems, everyone wants a friend. You don't have to look far. Anyone and everyone around you is a potential friend.

BE
RESPECTFUL

Respect is another word for feeling a sense of esteem, or recognizing the worth of someone or something. Everyone wants to be respected. Respect makes us feel happy, confident, and accomplished. Disrespect does the opposite. Since we all rely on other people, it's important that we're respectful to them. We must show those other people how much we value them. Being respectful is part of good citizenship because it's about understanding and acknowledging how much we need the people around us.

RESPECT IN ITS MANY FORMS

There are many different forms of respect. There is respect for our elders, like our parents, grandparents, aunts, uncles, teachers, and so on. We respect their depth of experience, their wisdom, their concern for our well-being, and all that they do for us. There is respect for our peers. We respect their feelings, their opinions, their bodies, and their property. There is respect for authority

SELF-RESPECT

Self-respect, also sometimes called self-esteem, doesn't mean bragging about how great you are. It also doesn't mean thinking you're perfect because no one is. Self-respect is about valuing yourself and the things you do. It's about knowing that you're important and having confidence in your abilities. In some respects, self-respect is even more crucial than respect for others. After all, how can you value someone else if you don't value yourself? Having self-respect also makes it more likely that others will respect you.

It isn't always easy to maintain our self-respect. There are a lot of reasons why we might feel bad about ourselves, like if we do poorly on a test or lose a friend. It's perfectly normal to have emotional ups and downs, but it's not OK to have low self-respect. It is unhealthy and can lead to very bad and dangerous decision making.

Here are some things to do if you think you have low self-esteem. First, make a list of the things you're good at. Maybe you're a talented artist or a good friend—we're all good at something. Second, don't put yourself down. Third, remember that there are things about each of us that we can't change, like our height, skin color, or the way we look. Accept the things that make you different from others because they are the things that make you special. If you're still having trouble, tell a trusted adult and consider seeking professional counseling.

and the law, which exist to protect us and everyone else in our community.

There are broader forms of respect as well. We shouldn't only respect the people we know, but all people. Are strangers undeserving of respect just because we don't know them? At some point in our lives, we didn't even know the people who became our best friends. All human beings deserve respect. We should also respect cultures and ethnicities other than our own. We live in a global society, and we rely on other countries and groups of people for trade, political alliances, humanitarian assistance, and culture. Broader still, we respect nature and all living things. All life is important, whether human, animal, or plant. We're deeply connected to the environment—it provides for us. We also respect concepts and ideas, like truth, kindness, justice, and freedom.

GETTING BACK WHAT YOU GIVE

Being respectful just means showing that we think a person or thing is important and acting accordingly. When we choose not to litter, we're respecting the environment. When we refrain from telling a lie, we're respecting other people's right to the truth and our own commitment to honesty. If you have respect in your heart, you will act in a respectful manner.

Why should we be respectful? When we're young, it's sometimes hard to respect older authority figures because we feel like they don't respect us. However, our parents and teachers do respect us, even if they don't give us all the freedom we'd like. Still if you feel like someone is disrespecting you, consider this—the only

Volunteers show respect for their community and the environment by picking up litter.

way for us to get respect is to give it. Look long and hard at your actions and make sure you're being respectful. Other people react to the way you treat them. If you disrespect them, it is likely they will disrespect you. You know what it's like to be disrespected, and it's not a good feeling, so work hard to respect others.

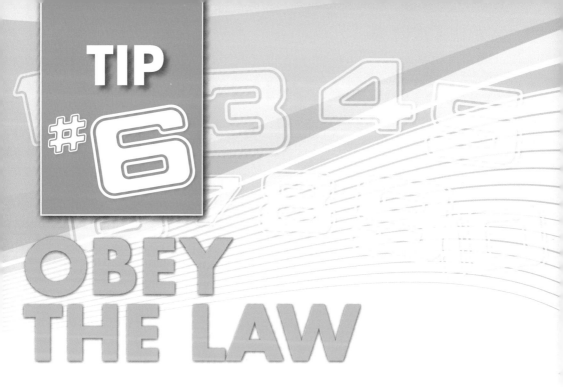

TIP #6

OBEY THE LAW

As citizens, we have an unspoken agreement, called the social contract or the social compact, with our government. The social contract says that we rely on our government for certain things, but it also means that our government relies on us. As citizens, we accept certain responsibilities, give up certain freedoms, and agree to follow the law in exchange for protection and services from the government. If we don't obey the law, we break our end of the social contract and forfeit our rights. It is important that we follow the social contract in order to maintain peace and order. There's no question about it: to be an ethical, good citizen, we must obey the law.

CRIME AND PUNISHMENT

We all know that if we're caught breaking the law, we will be punished. Punishments range in severity depending on the crime,

LAW AND CIVILIZATION

Systems of law have promoted the growth of civilization for thousands of years. In 3000 BCE, ancient Egypt had a civil code of law. King Hammurabi of Babylon inscribed his law code onto several stones spread around the region so that the general public could always see and be reminded of it. The Codex of Hammurabi, or Hammurabi's Code, is most famous for the phrase "an eye for an eye, a tooth for a tooth." That same sentiment is echoed in the Torah (the first five books of the Hebrew Bible and Christian Old Testament). The advanced civilizations of ancient Sumeria, Greece, Rome, India, Maya, Inca, and China all had legal codes that allowed them to expand and flourish. Can you imagine what life would be like without law? There'd be no peace, security, safety, art, science, or culture. In fact, without law there would be no civilization at all.

but any legal punishment would make our lives harder. After all, they wouldn't be punishments if they made our lives easier. In fact, punishments are designed to be bad enough so that people would think twice before they act in violation of the law. Maybe more people would steal cars if there was no punishment, but if they know that they could be put in prison for twenty years, they might think twice.

Depending on the crime, we could also be affected socially even after our punishment has ended. Ex-convicts often have a much harder time finding jobs once out of prison, and they aren't allowed to vote in many states. People in the general public are often reluctant to associate with ex-convicts, even though they've served their time. One crime committed in a moment of thoughtlessness or passion can ruin the rest of your life.

Juvenile offenders wait to be transferred to various detention facilities where they'll serve their sentences. Even minors can receive harsh punishments for violating the law.

THE PROTECTIVE POWER OF LAWS

There are reasons to obey the law besides fear of punishment. We take it for granted, but the law provides for us in many ways. First, it protects us from harm. If someone hurts you or your property, he or she will be punished. Second, the law promotes the common good. That means it protects citizens from situations in which an individual acting in his or her own narrow interest hurts the rest of society, even if that individual means no harm. For example, a corporation may exploit and damage the environment, which hurts us all, for personal profit. The law protects against that. Third, the law helps resolve disputes between members of a community. If two people disagree about something, they can go to court for a resolution.

It might not seem like it, but all laws are important. They're all in place for specific reasons, even if we don't realize what those reasons are. Speeding might not seem like a big deal, but speed limits protect pedestrians, cyclists, drivers, and passengers from accidental harm. The speed of a car involved in an accident could mean the difference between life and death. Also, breaking one law makes it easier to break more in the future. Most criminals start by breaking smaller laws. When they don't get caught, they feel like they can break bigger laws.

All laws serve a function, even if we're unaware of it. Obeying the law isn't just part of being an ethical, good citizen—it's the very definition of citizenship.

KNOW AND STAND UP FOR YOUR RIGHTS

Just as it's possible to be harmed by a person, it is also possible to be harmed by the government—governmental departments and agencies, school systems, courts, and police departments are made up of individual citizens, after all. It isn't always easy for politicians, government employees, law enforcement officials, or school teachers and administrators to set aside their personal biases when they go to work.

It is unfortunate, but there are certain situations in which an authority figure might abuse his or her power to take advantage of you. A police officer might wrongly assume you're guilty of a crime, for example, and violate your rights in order to prove it. A teacher could disagree with your opinions and try to prevent you from expressing them. Knowing your rights is the best way to protect yourself and others from abuse of authority.

INALIENABLE RIGHTS

Every human being has certain rights. The law provides some to citizens as a sort of privilege, while others are considered inalienable, universal, or "natural." This means that no one, not even the government, can take them away. The individual was born with these rights; they are a birthright of humanity and can't be violated or taken away by any earthly authority.

These citizens protest a U.S. Supreme Court decision that they believe opposes their inalienable rights by signing an enormous copy of the U.S. Constitution, the legal document that protects U.S. citizens' civil rights.

Authority figures can't violate your inalienable rights no matter how much power they have. Still, in certain cases they might do their best to lie to you about your rights or prey on ignorance. If you feel like your rights are being violated, don't just take someone's word for it. Do some research of your own. In the past, governments around the world have violated the rights of political opponents; prisoners and prisoners of war; immigrants; the physically and mentally impaired; women; gays and lesbians; and ethnic, racial, and religious minorities. Today, the law in most

CIVIL DISOBEDIENCE

Many civil rights movements have used civil disobedience to rebel against laws or practices that violate their rights. Civil disobedience is when an individual or group breaks a law in order to protest that law or some other injustice. Usually, civil disobedience is nonviolent. Practitioners spread public awareness by passively disobeying authority figures with boycotts, sit-ins, or picketing. American intellectual and author Henry David Thoreau first mentioned civil disobedience in 1849.

Most famously, Mohandas Gandhi used civil disobedience in the first half of the twentieth century to protest the British occupation of India. Gandhi's nonviolent protests led India to freedom and inspired others around the world, including Martin Luther King Jr. King used civil disobedience through sit-ins, the Montgomery Bus Boycott, and the famous March on Washington to protest America's persecution and unequal treatment of African-American citizens. Civil disobedience continues to be used around the world as an effective and nonviolent way to express frustration with unjust governments.

democracies protects their rights, but many authority figures still bring their personal prejudices to work. Minorities are still treated unfairly. Some minorities, like GLBT (gay, lesbian, bisexual, or transgendered) people, still don't have equal rights under the law in most places.

Citizens take part in a peaceful demonstration on legalizing same-sex marriage.

FIGHT FOR YOUR RIGHTS— AND THOSE OF OTHERS!

Being a good citizen is not passively obeying the government at the expense of the inalienable rights of oneself or others. Good citizens are proactive. They protect each other. By allowing authority figures to step on others, we create an unjust society that may one day exploit and repress us, too. It's important that we protect everyone's rights. We live in a society in which an injustice committed against one person represents an injustice to us all.

If you see or experience an injustice, do something about it. Document the situation by taking thorough notes with names, dates, and any other details you can think of. Get support from others who are in a similar situation. Obey the law, even if it seems unfair—breaking rules only gives your opponent ammunition against you. There are legal ways to get justice, like public demonstrations, petitions, a letter to a newspaper, a boycott, and the court system. Within the law, you can take action to ensure that everyone's universal rights are upheld.

MYTHS & FACTS

MYTH: YOU CAN BE SUSPENDED OR EXPELLED AT ANY TIME, FOR ANY REASON.

FACT: EVERY AMERICAN STUDENT HAS A LEGAL RIGHT TO PUBLIC EDUCATION. THAT MEANS SCHOOLS HAVE TO FOLLOW A CERTAIN PROCESS AND GIVE STUDENTS A CHANCE TO EXPLAIN AND DEFEND THEMSELVES.

MYTH: YOU'RE NOT ALLOWED TO SAY WHAT YOU WANT AT SCHOOL.

FACT: YOU HAVE THE RIGHT TO SELF-EXPRESSION, EVEN IN SCHOOL, SO LONG AS IT DOESN'T CAUSE A SIGNIFICANT DISRUPTION. YOU CAN'T YELL IN THE MIDDLE OF CLASS OR USE OFFENSIVE LANGUAGE, BUT AT THE PROPER TIMES, YOU CAN TALK TO YOUR FRIENDS, TEACHERS, OR PRINCIPAL ABOUT THE ISSUES THAT MATTER TO YOU MOST.

MYTH: YOUR TEACHERS CAN SAY WHATEVER THEY WANT TO YOU.

FACT: TEACHERS ARE NOT ALLOWED TO VERBALLY ABUSE THEIR STUDENTS.

TIP #8

KNOW YOUR HISTORY

In order to be an ethical citizen who is proactive, informed, respectful, responsible, happy, and self-confident, you have to know your history. History concerns things that have happened in the past. Since these events are past, it may seem like they're over, distant, and irrelevant. What do you care what someone did a hundred years ago? How could it possibly affect you?

Well, think, for instance, about the city you live in. You know how it is now, but how did it get to be the way it is? At one point, there was no city. A long time ago, people founded your city, and their lives and decisions, though they are long past, continue to determine your present. Where would you live if not for them, and under what alternate system of laws and cultural influences? History isn't just about things that have already happened—it's also about how past events are affecting the present and influencing the future.

THE PAST ILLUMINATES THE PRESENT AND FUTURE

We need to know history in order to make educated decisions in the present. History provides lessons on how to live effectively. We can draw on examples of what's worked in the past and what hasn't. For example, when designing new airplanes, aerospace engineers examine past designs to learn from past mistakes. After all, why make the same mistakes that someone else has already made? The same is true for everything from our daily lives to international conflicts—those who don't learn from history are said to be doomed to repeat the mistakes of the past.

Students watch footage of the Reverend Dr. Martin Luther King Jr.'s historic "I Have a Dream" speech at the Birmingham Civil Rights Museum in Alabama.

Current events and political issues are rooted deeply in the past. If we don't know history, we won't be able to understand why there's a revolution in the Middle East, a civil war in Africa, or a debt crisis in Europe. Without historical knowledge, we can't form educated opinions about the world today or be full participants in our government.

HISTORY AND PERSONAL IDENTITY

More personally, history is part of identity. How did your parents name you? How did they meet? When did your family come to this country, from where, and why? All of these things and more have partly made you who you are today, even though they happened in the past. If you don't know the answers to these questions, then you're missing crucial pieces of knowledge about your own identity.

Some past events have affected everyone, like the founding of our country for example. That means everyone in this country has a common history and a common identity to some extent. We've all been affected by the actions, efforts, thoughts, and words of our founding fathers. History teaches us that despite some differences in appearance, customs, traditions, and opinions, humans are more like each other than not. This awareness makes it easier to connect with other people, even those who, on a superficial level, seem most different from us.

Learn about your ethnicity, city, state, country, and the world. It's the only way to be a well-informed, proud, effective citizen.

MEDIA BIAS

It's impossible to be completely objective, but some media outlets are flat-out biased. This bias can often serve to highlight the differences among people and increase antagonism, rather than emphasize our similarities and common humanity, our shared goals and aspirations.

Why does this media bias exist? Most media sources, like newspapers, TV stations, or Web sites, rely on corporate advertisers for their money. They do their best to gain the biggest audience possible so that they can attract more advertisers and make more money. That approach doesn't always lead to the best reporting. Some media sources are actually owned by large companies that use the outlet for their own political or financial agendas. They spin or withhold information in order to shape public perception in their favor.

It's important to know that the media can be biased. Don't accept any information, historical accounts, or opinions at face value. Always be skeptical and ask questions. Get your information and history from many different sources so that you get a feel for the full range of opinions and perspectives before deciding what you believe is the truth.

Read books, watch documentaries, and visit history museums. If you're interested, you could even join a local historical society. Talk to your parents and grandparents. Ask them stories about when they were young. Did they grow up in your city or town, or somewhere else? What was it like? Why did they move? You might be surprised at how interesting their stories are and how relevant they are to your own life.

10 GREAT QUESTIONS
TO ASK A HISTORY TEACHER
ABOUT YOUR HOMETOWN

 WHO FOUNDED THE TOWN?

 WHY WAS IT FOUNDED?

 HOW DID THE FOUNDERS CHOOSE THE SPOT?

 HOW DID THE TOWN GET ITS NAME?

 HOW OLD IS THE TOWN?

 HOW MUCH HAS THE TOWN GROWN SINCE ITS FOUNDING?

 WHO DESIGNED THE TOWN'S PLAN AND LAYOUT?

 WHAT WAS THE TOWN'S MAIN SOURCE OF REVENUE AT VARIOUS POINTS IN HISTORY?

 WHAT WAS DAILY LIFE LIKE IN THE TOWN AT VARIOUS POINTS IN HISTORY?

 HOW HAS THE TOWN CHANGED PHYSICALLY, CULTURALLY, DEMOGRAPHICALLY, AND ECONOMICALLY?

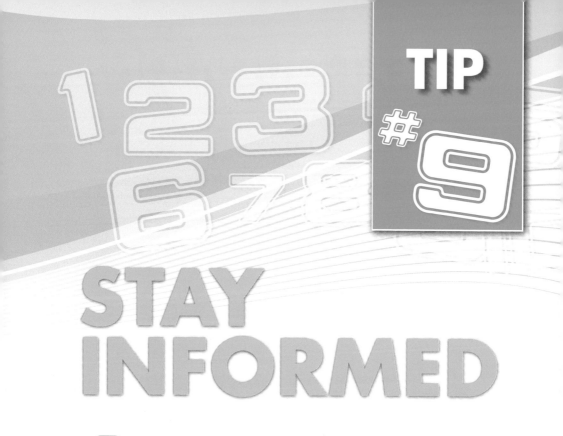

STAY INFORMED

A scientific advance makes your life easier. International conflict threatens global stability. Unseasonable weather damages crop production. Oil prices drive up the cost of goods. Do you know what's going on in the world today? You should.

We live in a global community in which other people's actions can, and do, drastically affect our daily lives. Unfortunately, many people live their lives in a fog, completely unaware of how they're being manipulated by governments, taken advantage of by other people, negatively impacted by the economy, and so on. To be good citizens, we have to stay informed. If we don't, we'll be unaware of the important issues that affect our daily lives, and we won't be able to prepare or react to things that could hurt us.

FOLLOW THE NEWS

If a hurricane were on track to hit your hometown, how would you know? Maybe someone else would tell you, likely your parents, but they must get their information from somewhere. The news media reports on everything that's happening in the world. Global, national, local, sports, business, and entertainment news—it's all covered on television, the radio, in print, and on the Internet.

Reading, watching, or listening to news might sometimes seem boring and dry, but knowing what's happening in the world allows you to make smarter personal decisions that benefit your life and the lives of those around you. Politicians and businesspeople make decisions every day that affect your future. When Congress makes a law that you disagree with or that will harm your interests, you can protest the law—unless, of course, you don't have enough information

Following the news is easier and more convenient than ever, thanks to technology.

to fully understand or even be aware of the issue. Every day, legislation is passed that the general public would find unfair, unpopular, and unjust if only they knew.

Use just a half an hour every day to watch, read, or listen to the news. Visit various sources with different viewpoints and analyze them so that you can form your own opinion. Different sources may not agree with each other, and you may not agree with them, but that's OK. Disagreement and informed debate are an extremely important part of democracy and can lead you to a

RESPECTFUL DISCUSSION OR CONTENTIOUS ARGUMENT?

There is nothing wrong with disagreeing with someone else. You should always feel comfortable voicing your opinion as long as you do so in a polite and respectful manner. Discussion, even if it gets animated, is a good path to understanding. However, you have to make sure to explore topics respectfully and avoid hurting other people's feelings.

There is a fine line between a respectful discussion and a contentious or antagonistic argument. Some people feel so strongly about certain subjects that they get emotional if others disagree with them. In fact, many people don't like to talk about current events, politics, or religion for fear of offending someone's sensibilities or being offended themselves. These can be very touchy subjects. An ideological disagreement can easily become a full-blown fight. That doesn't mean you shouldn't voice your opinion, though. The important thing is to keep a clear head and respect other people's opinions.

better understanding of a topic. If you have trouble understanding a topic or story, talk about it with your parents and teachers. Ask them questions. Discussing the news with others might be more interesting to you than just reading the news by yourself.

TAKE ACTION

It's not enough to be informed—you have to go out and use that information to your benefit and to the benefit of your community. No one is too young to know how current events are affecting his or her life. You can't vote, but you can still get involved. Volunteer with different political or issue-based organizations. Attend debates. Get in touch with your political representatives by calling or writing them. Go to town meetings. And if you disagree with something, voice your opin-

High school students register to vote. Voting is a basic right and responsibility.

ion. That's a crucial part of citizenship, yet it is a right that goes unused too often. Take control of your life, protect yourself and others, and use information as a tool.

GET INVOLVED!

Our community needs us, just like we need it. Democracy requires our input, not just through voting but also through participating. If we don't participate, our community will lose touch with our best interests. In order to be good citizens and ensure that we're protected, we have to get involved.

VOLUNTEERING

Volunteering is one of the most rewarding things you can do. Pledge your time to a local organization for a cause that you care about. Do you like animals? Help out at your local animal shelter. Do you enjoy playing sports? Try assisting a sports league for younger kids. Want to get a candidate elected for mayor? Join the campaign. These organizations will welcome your help, and by

Students from a high school leadership class volunteer at a food bank in Cleveland, Ohio.

choosing an organization you're interested in, you can be sure that you'll enjoy it and feel good about helping others. Volunteering is also an excellent way to make friends with people who share similar interests. It also reflects well on your résumé when you eventually apply for jobs or college admission.

THINK LOCAL, ACT LOCAL

Many people take the place they live for granted. They live their lives without knowing what's special about their local community.

TECHNOLOGY MAKES TAKING ACTION EASY

The Internet and digital tools like smartphones, tablets, and social networking Web sites are invaluable aids for getting involved. They can help you gather information, organize events, spread a message, and find people and groups with interests similar to yours.

In fact, new media technologies have recently played an extremely important role in enacting social changes around the world. Social networking sites like Facebook and Twitter actually helped people in Tunisia, Libya, Yemen, and Egypt organize popular protests in 2011 that eventually overthrew their oppressive rulers. Civil uprisings, facilitated in part by social networking and Internet technology, also occurred in Bahrain, Iraq, Syria, Algeria, Jordan, Kuwait, Morocco, Oman, Lebanon, Mauritania, Saudi Arabia, Sudan, and the Palestinian territories.

The Arab Spring, as the series of Middle Eastern revolts and revolutions are being called, has made the entire world aware of technology's potential role in citizen action. Technology makes organizing people and taking action easier and more effective.

Every city and town is interesting and special in its own right. See what activities your community has to offer, and go out and enjoy them. Does your town have a great beach? Maybe there's a beautiful park, a library, or a museum. Take advantage of where you live. As you get to know your community, your pride in it will grow. And you'll enjoy yourself in the process.

As you become more familiar with your community, think about how it could improve. No place is perfect, but your community could come close. Think about your idea of the perfect community, and do your best to make it a reality. What's it missing? Should there be more parks? Should there be more bike lanes or bike paths? Help make your community the best it can be. If something is wrong, do your best to fix it or convince those in a position of power to make the changes you seek. Remember, you can only make things better by getting involved.

Youth shouldn't hold you back. No one is too young, and no one is too old. We can all take action to promote change and make our community a better place for everyone. By getting involved, you might even inspire someone else, like your friends or your parents. That spirit of good citizenship will continue to spread. Lead by example. As Gandhi once said, "Be the change you want to see."

BIAS A prejudice, inclination, or tendency that prevents objectivity.

CITIZEN An inhabitant of a city, state, or nation who is entitled to protection and other services in exchange for upholding certain responsibilities.

CITIZENSHIP The state of having the rights, privileges, and responsibilities of a citizen.

CIVIL DISOBEDIENCE The refusal to obey laws in order to protest government policy, usually through nonviolent means like boycotting, picketing, or petitioning.

COMMON GOOD The good that is shared by all; what is beneficial to the community or population as a whole.

COMMUNITY A unified body of individuals; a group of people with common interests or characteristics living in a particular area within the larger society.

CONSEQUENCE The effect or outcome of something that occurred earlier.

ETHICS Guiding moral principles.

GOLDEN RULE An ethical precept that says one should treat others as one would treat oneself.

HISTORY A chronological record of significant events, often including an explanation of their causes.

INALIENABLE RIGHTS Also called natural rights, they're self-evident or universal rights that are shared by all people and that no government or authority can take away.

INTENTION The reason someone does something; the purpose or motivation behind an action.

LAW The body of rules established in a community that pertains to all citizens.

MORALS Rules of conduct.

NEIGHBOR A person who lives near another. More broadly, a person who shows kindness and helpfulness toward his or her fellow human beings.

RECIPROCITY A state of mutual exchange.

RESPECT Esteem for another person, place, thing, or idea.

SELF-EXPRESSION The assertion, or expression, of one's personality or self through behavior, conversation, personal appearance, writing, singing, dancing, art, or other means.

SELF-RESPECT Esteem for the quality of one's own character, intelligence, health, and well-being.

SOCIAL CONTRACT Also called the social compact, it explains the relationship between individual citizens and their government, in which citizens trade certain rights and freedoms in order to gain others, and in which the government offers certain rights, freedoms, protections, and services in exchange for loyalty, social order, and payment of taxes, among other things.

American Civil Liberties Union (ACLU)
125 Broad Street, 18th Floor
New York, NY 10004
(212) 549-2500
Web site: http://www.aclu.org
The ACLU views itself as the nation's guardian of liberty,
    working daily in courts, legislatures, and communities
    to defend and preserve the individual rights and
    liberties that the Constitution and laws of the United
    States guarantee everyone in this country. These
    rights include free speech, freedom of the press,
    freedom of association and assembly, freedom of
    religion, freedom from discrimination, the right to
    due process, and the right to privacy.

American Ethical Union
2 West 64th Street
New York, NY 10023
(212) 873-6500
Web site: http://aeu.org
Ethical Culture is a humanistic religious and educational
    movement inspired by the idea that the supreme aim
    of human life is working to create a more humane
    society.

Boys and Girls Clubs of Canada
7100 Woodbine Avenue, Suite 204
Markham, ON L3R 5J2

Canada
(905) 477-7272
Web site: http://www.bgccan.com
This organization provides places where youth can form
new relationships and learn skills for adult life.

Center for Constitutional Rights (CCR)
666 Broadway, 7th Floor
New York, NY 10012
(212) 614-6464
Web site: http://ccrjustice.org
The CCR is dedicated to advancing and protecting the
rights guaranteed by the U.S. Constitution and the
Universal Declaration of Human Rights.

Do Something, Inc.
24-32 Union Square East, 4th Floor
New York, NY 10003
(212) 254-2390, ext. 236
Web site: http://www.dosomething.org
Do Something believes young people everywhere can
improve their communities. It leverages communi-
cations technologies to enable youths to convert
their ideas and energy into action. Its aim is to
inspire, empower, and celebrate a generation of
doers: young people who recognize the need to do
something, believe in their ability to get it done,
and then take action.

First Amendment Center
555 Pennsylvania Avenue
Washington, DC 20001
(202) 292-6288
Web site: http://www.firstamendmentcenter.org
The First Amendment Center supports the First
    Amendment and builds understanding of its core
    freedoms through education, information, and enter-
    tainment. The center serves as a forum for the study
    and exploration of free expression issues, including
    freedom of speech, the press, and religion, and the
    rights to assemble and petition the government.

Freedom Forum
555 Pennsylvania Avenue NW
Washington, DC 20001
(202) 292-6100
Web site: http://www.freedomforum.org
The Freedom Forum, based in Washington, D.C., is a
    nonpartisan foundation that champions the First
    Amendment as a cornerstone of democracy. The
    Freedom Forum is the main funder of the operations
    of the Newseum, also in Washington, D.C.; the First
    Amendment Center; and the Diversity Institute.

Human Rights Watch (HRW)
350 Fifth Avenue, 34th Floor

New York, NY 10118-3299
(212) 290-4700
Web site: http://www.hrw.org

The HRW is dedicated to protecting the human rights of people around the world. It stands with victims and activists to prevent discrimination, uphold political freedom, protect people from inhumane conduct in wartime, and bring offenders to justice. It investigates and exposes human rights violations and holds abusers accountable. The HRW challenges governments and those who hold power to end abusive practices and respect international human rights law. It enlists the public and the international community to support the cause of human rights for all.

People for the American Way
2000 M Street NE, Suite 400
Washington, DC 20036
(202) 467-4999
Web site: http://www.pfaw.org

People for the American Way is dedicated to making the promise of America real for every American, in part by working to ensure equality, freedom of speech, freedom of religion, the right to seek justice in a court of law, and the right to cast a vote that counts. Its vision of America is of a nation and a people that respect diversity, nurture creativity, and combat hatred and bigotry.

Scouts Canada
1345 Baseline Road
Ottawa, ON K2C 0A7
Canada
(888) 726-8876
Web site: http://www.scouts.ca
This youth organization uses outdoor activity to teach
   ethical living and good citizenship.

WEB SITES

Due to the changing nature of Internet links, Rosen Publishing has developed an online list of Web sites related to the subject of this book. This site is updated regularly. Please use this link to access the list:

http://www.rosenlinks.com/top10/ctzn

FOR FURTHER READING

Bailey, Diane. *Cyber Ethics* (Cyber Citizenship and Cyber Safety). New York, NY: Rosen Central, 2008.

Bellamy, Richard. *Citizenship: A Very Short Introduction.* New York, NY: Oxford University Press, 2008.

Blackburn, Simon. *Ethics: A Very Short Introduction.* New York, NY: Oxford University Press, 2009.

Maury, Rob. *Citizenship: Rights and Responsibilities.* Broomall, PA: Mason Crest, 2007.

McNeese, Tim. *The Civil Rights Movement: Striving for Justice* (Reform Movements in American History). New York, NY: Chelsea House, 2007.

Nouraee, Andisheh, Daniel Ehrenhaft, and Jodi Lynn Anderson. *Americapedia: Taking the Dumb Out of Freedom.* New York, NY: Walker, 2011.

Panza, Christopher, and Adam Potthast. *Ethics for Dummies.* Hoboken, NJ: For Dummies, 2010.

Rappaport, Doreen. *Martin's Big Words: The Life of Dr. Martin Luther King, Jr.* New York, NY: Hyperion Books, 2007.

Selzer, Adam. *The Smart Aleck's Guide to American History.* New York, NY: Delacorte Books for Young Readers, 2009.

Vigliano, Adrian. *Being a Good Citizen.* Mankato, MN: Heinemann-Raintree, 2009.

Wales, Jenny. *Citizenship Today.* Glasgow, Scotland: Collins Educational, 2009.

BIBLIOGRAPHY

Aleinikoff, T. Alexander, and Douglas B. Klusmeyer, eds. *Citizenship Today: Global Perspectives and Practices.* Washington, DC: Carnegie Endowment for International Peace, 2001.

Biography.com. "Mahatma Gandhi Biography." Retrieved October 2011 (http://www.biography.com/people/mahatma-gandhi-9305898).

Cahn, Steven M., and Peter Markie, eds. *Ethics: History, Theory, and Contemporary Issues.* New York, NY: Oxford University Press, 2008.

Kids.gov. "Government: Citizen's Rights and Responsibilities." October 7, 2011. Retrieved October 2011 (http://www.kids.gov/6_8/6_8_government_rights.shtml).

KidsHealth.org. "The Story of Self-Esteem." Retrieved October 2011 (http://kidshealth.org/kid/feeling/emotion/self_esteem.html).

MacKinnon, Barbara. *Ethics: Theory and Contemporary Issues.* Belmont, CA: 2012.

Marino, Gordon. *Ethics: The Essential Writings.* New York, NY: Modern Library, 2010.

Maxwell, John C. *Ethics 101: What Every Leader Needs to Know.* New York, NY: Center Street, 2005.

NobelPrize.org. "Martin Luther King: Biography." Retrieved October 2011 (http://www.nobelprize.org/nobel_prizes/peace/laureates/1964/king-bio.html).

Parker-Pope, Tara. "What Are Friends For? A Longer Life." *New York Times*, April 20, 2009. Retrieved

October 2011 (http://www.nytimes.com/2009/04/21/
  health/21well.html).
Patel, Samir S. "Why Loneliness Is Bad for You."
  Discover Magazine, January 15, 2008. Retrieved
  October 2011 (http://discovermagazine.com/2008/
  jan/why-loneliness-is-bad-for-you).
Stanford Encyclopedia of Philosophy. "Citizenship."
  Stanford University, July 9, 2009. Retrieved October
  2011 (http://plato.stanford.edu/entries/citizenship).
Stanford Encyclopedia of Philosophy. "Friendship."
  Stanford University, July 9, 2009. Retrieved October
  2011 (http://plato.stanford.edu/entries/friendship).
Stanford Encyclopedia of Philosophy. "Philosophy of
  History." Stanford University, July 21, 2010.
  Retrieved October 2011 (http://plato.stanford.edu/
  entries/history).
Stanford Encyclopedia of Philosophy. "Respect."
  Stanford University, July 21, 2010. Retrieved October
  2011 (http://plato.stanford.edu/entries/respect).
Stanford Encyclopedia of Philosophy. "Rights." Stanford
  University, July 21, 2010. Retrieved October 2011
  (http://plato.stanford.edu/entries/rights).
Vila, Susannah. "Social Media and Satire Fuel Arab
  Spring in Tunisia, Egypt." PBS.org, July 14, 2011.
  Retrieved October 20, 2011 (http://www.pbs.org/
  mediashift/2011/07/social-media-and-satire-fuel-
  arab-spring-in-tunisia-egypt195.html).

INDEX

ABOUT THE AUTHOR

Joe Craig has written previously about contemporary issues, friendship and dating, and other teen concerns. He lives in Queens, New York.

PHOTO CREDITS

Cover istockphoto.com/Steve Debenport; pp. 5, 14 © AP Images; p. 8 Michael S. Gordon/The Republican/ Landov; p. 17 Kansas City Star/McClatchy-Tribune/Getty Images; p. 19 istockphoto.com/Randolph Pamphrey; p. 22 Brendan O'Sullivan/Photolibrary/Getty Images; p. 23 Yellow Dog Productions/Stone/Getty Images; p. 28 UniversalImagesGroup/Getty Images; p. 31 © Larry Kolvoord/The Image Works; p. 34 Chip Somodevilla/ Getty Images; p. 36 Kevork Djansezian/Getty Images; p. 40 © St. Petersburg Times/ZUMA Press; p. 45 © pixelbully/Alamy; p. 47 © Scott Threlkeld/The Times-Picayune/Landov; p. 49 © Chuck Crow/The Plain Dealer/ Landov; interior background graphic, back cover phyZick/ Shutterstock.com.

Designer: Nicole Russo; Photo Researcher: Amy Feinberg